For kids everywhere, that they may find
wonder and joy in being themselves
—C.B.C.

To Liam and Aya, whose genuine laughter
always makes me HAPPY
—H.K.

Text copyright © 2018 by Courtney Carbone
Cover art and interior illustrations copyright © 2018 by Hilli Kushnir

Visit us on the Web! rhcbooks.com

Educators and librarians, for a variety of teaching tools, visit us at
RHTeachersLibrarians.com

Library of Congress Cataloging-in-Publication Data is available upon request.
ISBN 978-1-63565-057-0 (hardcover) — ISBN 978-1-63565-039-6 (ebook)
ISBN 978-1-63565-038-9 (pbk.)

MANUFACTURED IN CHINA
10 9 8 7 6 5 4 3
First Edition

This Makes Me Happy

RODALE KiDS

Today my class is going on
a field trip to the county fair!

We are all so excited!
It is hard to stay in our seats.

My teacher shows us
one way to relax.

We breathe in slowly.
We breathe out slowly.
Now I feel calm.

We get to the fair.
There is so much
to see and do!

I am so excited.
It feels like there are
butterflies in my tummy!

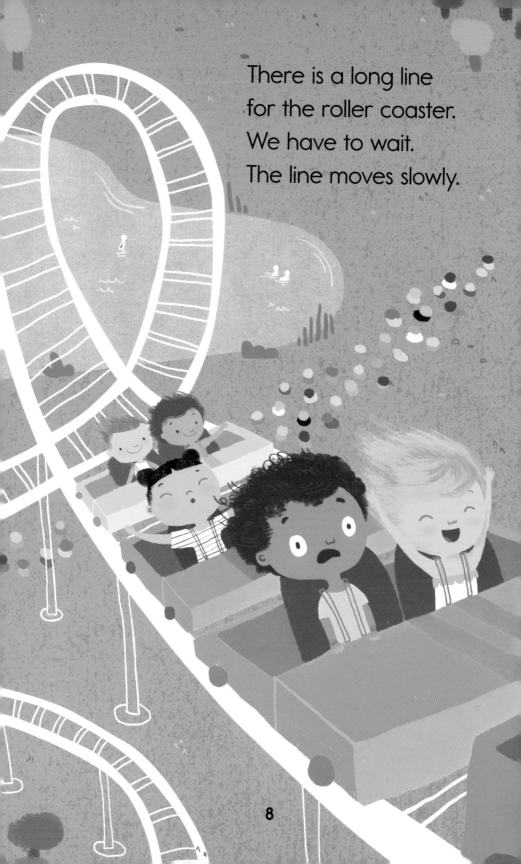

There is a long line
for the roller coaster.
We have to wait.
The line moves slowly.

But the ride is
worth the wait.
We go so fast.
I feel like I am flying!

Next, I get my face painted.
I ask the artist to paint
a yellow sun on my cheek.

She gives the sun
a big smile to match
the one on my face.

There is a pie-eating contest.
My teacher enters.

Three! Two! One!
The whistle blows.
We cheer her on.

She wins!
We jump up and down.

We see a glass jar
full of jelly beans.
It is a guessing game!

14

The jelly beans are every color of the rainbow. It feels like there is a rainbow inside of me, too!

15

Then we go
to the petting zoo.

We help the farmer
feed the animals.
They tickle our hands.
I can't stop laughing!

We get to see a chick
hatch from her shell.

She is so small!
Cheep! Cheep!

The chick makes me feel
big and strong.
I can do anything!

There is a bake sale to support a good cause.

But I am allergic to nuts.
I cannot eat any
of the treats.

I feel left out.
My teacher sits
down next to me.
She has allergies, too.

She tells me not to worry.
We can still help out.
She is right!

It is time to go home.
We walk back to the bus
hand in hand.

What a great day!
My heart feels
like a hot air balloon
high in the sky.

I have a good feeling
in my tummy.

But I did not have any treats!
What gave me this feeling?

Going on rides
was exciting.

Playing games was a lot of fun.

Helping others made me feel good.

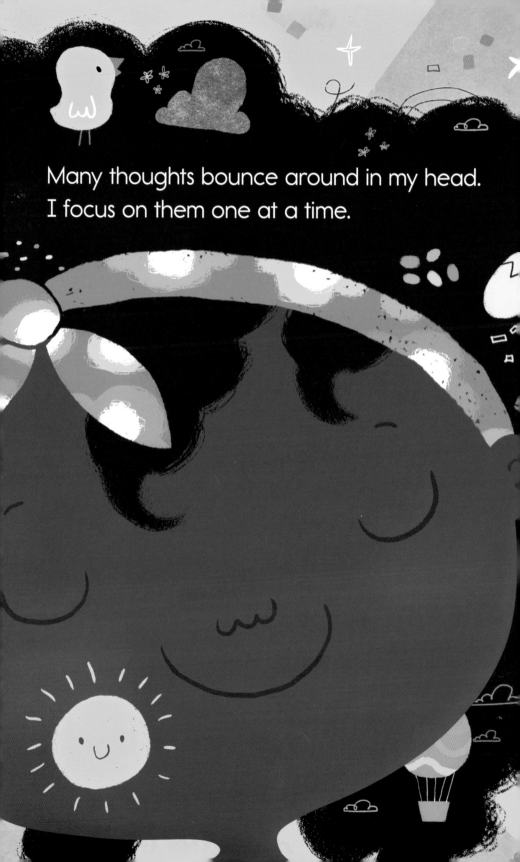

Many thoughts bounce around in my head.
I focus on them one at a time.

What am I feeling?
I am feeling HAPPY.

What makes **YOU** happy?

Also available:

  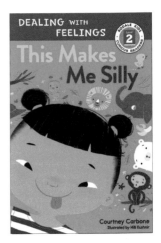

Look for these other titles in the
DEALING WITH FEELING series:
- **This Makes Me Sad**
- **This Makes Me Angry**
- **This Makes Me Silly**
- **This Makes Me Scared**
- **This Makes Me Jealous**

To learn more about Rodale Kids Curious Readers,
please visit RodaleKids.com.